V A BROWNING

Claimed By the Shadow Sentinel

SHADOW BOUND MATES #1

Contents

Read More here: books.vabrowing.com

1

Code Red

Maya

The third gas explosion victim coded at 11:47 PM, and I was elbow-deep in another patient's chest cavity.

"Maya, Bay Four's crashing!" Jen's voice cut through the chaos.

"Busy." I pressed both hands against the arterial bleed. "Get Torres."

"Torres is in surgery. You're it."

Of course I was.

The ER smelled like blood, antiseptic, and desperation. Another Tuesday in Minneapolis.

"He's stable for transport." I pulled back, letting the surgical resident take over. "Bay Four. What am I walking into?"

Jen matched my stride. "John Doe, brought in forty minutes ago. Burns and lacerations. Should be critical, but his vitals are stable. Too stable. Maya, this guy came in looking like he fell into a furnace."

I shouldered through the curtain into Bay Four.

John Doe sat upright on the gurney. Wrong. Severe burn victims don't sit upright.

"Finally." His pupils dilated wrong—too slow, then too fast. "I need to leave."

"You need treatment." I pulled on fresh gloves. "Can you tell me your name?"

"John."

"Last name?"

"Doe."

Funny. "I'm Dr. Reeves. Let me look at those burns."

His arms were a mess. Second and third-degree burns, lacerations on his chest. The wounds gaped raw and angry.

Except.

I leaned closer. The edges of the burns were changing. Pink skin creeping inward over damaged tissue. Like watching a time-lapse video of healing compressed into seconds.

Right. Hour twenty of my shift. Patients start healing like video game characters. I needed more coffee. Or an exorcist.

"Who else saw me come in?" John Doe's voice went tight. "How many people?"

"What?" I pulled back.

"Witnesses." His hand shot out, grabbed my wrist. Strong. Too strong. "Who saw my injuries?"

"Sir, I need you to let go—"

"Tell me."

The curtain ripped aside.

A guy built like a tactical refrigerator walked into my ER. Six-foot-four, shoulders that blocked the fluorescent light, all black tactical gear. Short black hair, military-precise. And his eyes—

Silver. Actual silver, catching the overhead lights like mirrors.

He moved through the ER like he was invisible. The nurse at the station glanced up, then away, her gaze sliding off him like water off glass.

"Let her go." Low voice. Command, not request.

John Doe's grip tightened. "Sentinel."

The word meant nothing to me. The way he said it meant everything—recognition, fear, hatred wrapped into two syllables.

The silver-eyed man stepped closer. I caught movement on his forearms. Tattoos that writhed and shifted under his skin like living shadows.

My brain refused to process what I was seeing.

"She's not part of this." His gaze locked onto mine.

Something happened.

I felt it in my chest—a hook through my ribcage, a pull toward him that made no sense. His eyes widened. The shadows on his arms went still, then surged toward me like they had minds of their own.

"You didn't see anything unusual." His voice dropped into something velvet and dark. "Go back to your other patients."

"Sorry, did you just try to Jedi mind trick me?" I yanked my arm free from John Doe's slack grip. "In my ER? Hard pass."

The silver-eyed man went absolutely still. "Impossible." His silver eyes went wide. His living tattoos seemed to shrink back in secondhand embarrassment.

John Doe's eyes snapped open. Wide. Wrong. The pupils had turned yellow, bleeding color into the whites like ink in water.

"Witness." His voice came out flat. Mechanical. "Eliminate."

He lunged.

One second he was on the gurney. The next his hands were around my throat, lifting me off the ground. My feet kicked empty air. My vision tunneled.

Can't breathe. Can't—

Darkness exploded across the room.

Living shadows ripped John Doe away from me. I hit the ground hard, gasping, throat on fire. Through watering eyes I watched the silver-eyed man's tattoos pour off his body—actual shadows made solid, wrapping around the patient like chains.

John Doe snarled and thrashed. The shadows held.

The man in black moved with predatory grace. Something glinted in his hand—a syringe. He drove it into John Doe's neck. The thrashing stopped.

"Maya."

I flinched. "How do you know my—"

"We need to move." He crouched beside me, silver eyes scanning my face, my throat. His jaw flexed. The shadows writhed around us both, brushing against my arms, my shoulders. Gentle. Curious.

Like they were tasting me.

"You're bleeding." His voice went rough.

My hand came up to my neck. Warm wetness. John Doe's nails had broken skin.

The man's nostrils flared. His whole body went rigid.

"Mine," he growled, then clamped his jaw shut, looking as if he'd just accidentally confessed to a love for boy bands.

"What—"

His head snapped toward the window. "Get down!"

He tackled me to the ground. His body covered mine—heavy, solid, smelling of leather and something darker. His shadows wrapped around us both like a cocoon.

The world exploded.

Glass shattered. The wall buckled. Heat and pressure and noise so loud it erased thought. I screamed into his chest while chaos tore through Bay Four.

Then silence.

Ringing silence. Smoke and dust and somewhere, someone screaming.

The man pulled back. His face was cut—glass shrapnel—but the wounds were already closing. Knitting together like John Doe's burns had.

"What are you?" My voice came out shredded.

"You're coming with me." He stood, hauled me up. "It's not safe here."

"I have patients—"

"They'll kill you to cover this up. Everyone who saw him." He jerked his chin toward John Doe's unconscious form. "That bomb wasn't random."

"You're insane. Let go of me."

His grip didn't budge. "I'm trying to save your life."

"My hero. The one who kidnaps me from my job."

"It's more efficient than asking nicely."

"I'm going to kick you."

"Noted." His silver eyes met mine. Something flickered in them. Regret, maybe. Or hunger. "I'm sorry."

The shadows swallowed us whole.

Cold. Dark. Falling through ice water, through nothing, through the space between heartbeats. I couldn't see, couldn't breathe, couldn't feel anything except the man's arms locked around me and the terrible certainty that I was dying.

Then my knees hit concrete.

I collapsed forward, heaving. Dim light. High ceilings. The smell of old metal and leather.

Not the hospital.

"What did you—" The words scraped out. I twisted around, scrambling backward. "Where is this?"

The man stood over me. Shadows pooled at his feet like obedient dogs. Behind him, rough brick walls, exposed beams. An industrial warehouse converted into living quarters.

"You're safe here."

"I was safe at work!"

"No." He crouched. "You weren't. You haven't been safe since the moment you walked into that patient's room."

My throat burned. My hands shook. My mother's bangles clinked as I pressed them against my chest. I surged to my feet, vision swimming, but stayed upright through sheer stubborn will. "You can't keep me here."

"I can." The shadows at his feet rose like a tide. "And I will. Until I find the rogue who's hunting you, you're not leaving my sight."

"That's kidnapping."

"It's a non-consensual protective extraction."

I stared at his retreating back as he moved deeper into the warehouse. At the shadows that trailed him like a cloak.

At the impossible reality of this moment—standing in a stranger's warehouse, throat bruised, scrubs stained with blood, having just learned that someone wanted me dead.

"Why?" The question scraped out. "Why save me? Out of everyone in that ER—why me?"

He stopped. His shoulders went rigid.

The shadows around him stilled. Then, slowly, they began to move toward me again. Stretching across the concrete. Reaching for my ankles, my wrists, my face. Not threatening. Yearning.

"Because you can't be compelled." His voice dropped to something rough and raw. "When I tried to make you forget, nothing happened. That shouldn't be possible."

"What does that mean?"

He turned back. Silver eyes burning.

"I'm a vampire, over 300 years old. We search through our lives for a Shadow Twin and you are mine." The words fell like stones. "My fated mate. The one person in existence who my powers can't touch. Someone who is a perfect match for eternity."

The shadows wrapped around my wrist. Gentle. Warm.

Like a lover's hand.

He took a step closer. "And it means I will burn down this entire city before I let anyone hurt you."

I stood there in that cold warehouse, surrounded by living darkness, the taste of fear and blood and impossible truth coating my tongue. My whole world had shattered in under an hour. And the man who'd shattered it watched me with silver eyes full of hunger, and grief, and a possessive certainty that terrified me more than anything else I'd seen tonight.

"Okay," I said, my voice surprisingly steady. "Then sit down. We have a lot to discuss."

I gestured toward a worn leather couch. "Let me get this straight. You're a vampire."

His posture was rigid. "Correct."

"And that guy was a thrall. Like, from Dungeons & Dragons?"

"I don't know what that is."

"Of course you don't." I waved a hand. "And now you've kidnapped me because I'm your Shadow Twin?"

"Yes."

"Is that like a participation trophy? Do I get a certificate?"

A long, pained silence stretched between us. "This is not a time for levity."

"Buddy," I shot back, "if I don't laugh at this, I'm going to start screaming, and trust me, you don't want that. My scream can shatter glass."

2
Shadow Bound

MAYA

A muscle feathered in his jaw. The kind of jaw that could cut glass, and wasn't that just perfect—kidnapped by a man who looked like he'd been carved from marble and malice.

"A vampire," I repeated. Right. A vampire. Who looks like he models for 'Brooding Monthly' and has sentient tattoos. This is fine. Everything is fine.

"Yes."

"With living tattoos."

"Shadow magic. Specific to House Adamas."

Is that like the House of Gucci? Do they have a signature scent? Malice and poor communication skills, probably.

"And you've been alive for... what was it? Three hundred and change?"

"Three hundred and forty-seven years."

I pressed my fingers to my temples. My bangles clinked. "You're older than the United States."

"Most things are."

"Was that a joke? Are you capable of jokes?"

"It's supposed to be factual."

I paced, running shoes squeaking against concrete. Step, squeak, breathe. Step, squeak, don't scream. My scrubs were still stiff with blood. My throat throbbed where a dead-eyed patient had tried to crush my windpipe.

"Start from the beginning. All of it."

The corner of his mouth twitched. "Vampires were created by Nyx. Goddess of night."

"You're starting with mythology."

"I'm starting with truth."

I dropped onto the couch arm. Perching, ready to bolt. "Fine. Goddess of night. Go on."

He stood with his back to the weapons rack, arms crossed. The shadow tattoos had settled into slow, lazy patterns along his forearms. Almost calm.

"Nyx blessed the first of our kind. The blessing passes through blood—either at birth or through conversion."

"Conversion. You mean turning someone."

"Yes."

"How?"

"Vampire blood introduced to the human system, followed by complete exsanguination. The mortal dies. If the virus takes hold, they wake."

My doctor brain snagged on every word. "What's the success rate?"

He paused. "High. Not guaranteed."

"That's not an answer."

"Ninety-three percent."

"And the other seven?"

"Stay dead."

I filed that away. Somewhere between terrifying and clinically fascinating. "Blood requirements. Frequency, volume, source."

His head tilted. "You're taking notes."

"I'm a doctor. This is a pathology I've never encountered. Talk."

Something shifted in his expression. "Blood sustains us. Bagged blood preferred—acquired through legal channels. Feeding from humans is discouraged. Daily requirement initially for new vampires, weekly for established ones. Volume comparable to a standard blood donation."

I pressed my palms flat on my thighs. Stopped them from shaking. "The patient in Bay Four. John Doe."

"He was a thrall. Corrupted."

"Like, from a video game? Does he drop loot when you kill him?"

Kael's jaw tightened. "There are legal thralls—humans in consensual blood bond contracts. It's regulated."

"Oh, good. The vampire underworld has an HR department."

He paced a short, angry line. "Then there are the illegal ones. Silas uses blood magic to strip their free will, turning them into programmable weapons. They get super strength, feel no pain, and burn out their own organs in weeks." He pinned me with his silver gaze. "He was a living bomb, and you were standing at ground zero."

"He was programmed to kill anyone who saw him."

"Yes."

"And the explosion at the hospital—"

"The rogue cleaning evidence. Everyone who treated that thrall is a target."

My stomach dropped. "Are they—"

"My people are handling it. Memory alteration for those who can be reached. Protection details for those at highest risk."

"Memory alteration. You can just erase people's minds?"

"Compulsion. Mental suggestion. Humans are susceptible."

"But not me."

The shadows on his arms went very still. "I can't compel you."

I touched my throat. "You tried. In the ER. You told me to forget and go back to my patients."

"And you told me to—how did you put it—'hard pass.'"

"So I'm immune to vampire mind control."

"You're immune to my compulsion. That's the distinction." He took a step forward. "Every vampire can influence human minds. But when a vampire encounters their Shadow Twin—their fated mate—the compulsion fails. It's the primary recognition signal. In three centuries, I've compelled thousands of humans. Not one has ever resisted."

"Until me."

"Until you."

The pull was there again. That hook-through-the-ribcage sensation, dragging me toward him like gravity had picked a favorite. I gripped the couch arm harder.

"I don't believe in fate."

"Fate doesn't require your belief."

"Poetic. Also obnoxious."

His shadows rippled. "The bond is biological. Chemical. Your doctor mind should appreciate that. Pheromone recognition, neural pathway synchronization—"

"Now you sound like a textbook."

"I'm trying to speak your language."

"My language is 'let me go home.'"

The silence that followed had weight. Kael's hand moved to his pocket, pulled out a phone. Not his—mine. I recognized the cracked case.

"This fell from your pocket during transport."

I snatched it. The screen lit up. Seventeen missed calls from Raj. A news notification sat at the top.

BREAKING: Gas Explosion Destroys South Minneapolis Apartment Complex. 14 Units Affected. Residents Evac uated.

The photo showed my building. What remained of it. The upper floors had collapsed inward, brick and siding peeled back like something had taken a bite.

My apartment was on the third floor. Corner unit. The corner that no longer existed.

"That happened 30 minutes after I brought you here. Staged to look like a gas leak. The rogue is eliminating every trace."

My mother's recipe box. The framed photo from her residency graduation. The silk scarf she wore on Diwali that still smelled like her perfume.

Gone.

My legs stopped working. I slid off the couch arm, knees hitting concrete, and Kael was there. Crouching in front of me, hands hovering at my shoulders, not touching. His shadows poured across the floor and wrapped around my ankles, my wrists, my hunched back. Warm. Gentle. The pressure of an embrace from something that wasn't quite alive but understood grief.

"Everything I had left of her was in that apartment."

Kael didn't ask who. The shadows tightened—not constraining, holding.

I breathed. In through the nose, out through the mouth. Trauma response management. Funny how it didn't work when the trauma was yours.

"Okay." I pressed my palms to the concrete. "So someone destroyed my apartment to kill me. A vampire someone."

"A rogue named Silas Mordain. Exiled from his House fifty years ago for illegal thrall experiments. He's building an army. You saw evidence of that army. He wants you dead."

"And you want me alive."

"More than I've wanted anything in three hundred and forty-seven years. I need you to stay here and be safe. Give me three days to find the rogue and show you what a Shadow Twin is."

His silver eyes held mine and I saw it—the loneliness behind the soldier. Three and a half centuries of empty rooms and nobody waiting for him to come home.

I recognized that look. I saw it in my bathroom mirror every morning.

I wiped my face. Not crying. Just—eyes leaking from smoke inhalation.

"I'm not hiding in your warehouse."

His jaw set. "It's the safest—"

"Safest, sure. But I'm not a piece of evidence you lock in a vault. If this rogue is hunting me, I'd rather know how to fight back than sit here hoping your shadow puppets keep the bad guys out."

"They're not puppets."

"They're nuzzling my elbow right now."

He glanced down. A tendril of shadow was, in fact, curled around my elbow, pulsing with something that felt embarrassingly close to affection. Kael's expression suggested he hadn't authorized this.

"They like you," he said through gritted teeth.

"Great. Your tattoos have a crush on me. Teach me to fight."

"No."

"That wasn't a request."

"You're human. Fragile. Mortal." Each word dropped like a stone. "Silas has killed vampires older and stronger than me. Training you won't—"

"Won't what? Won't make me invincible? Shocking. I don't need to be invincible. I need to not be helpless."

He paced to the weapons rack and back. His shadows trailed behind him, agitated. "If something happens to you—"

"If something happens to me while I'm locked in a room, you'll never forgive yourself. If something happens to me in a fight where I at least had a chance, you'll still never forgive yourself, but at least I'll have had a choice in it."

He stopped. Turned. Those silver eyes cut through the dim light.

"You've known me less than two hours and you already—"

"Know that you'd rather die protecting me than let me take a single risk? Yeah. I've met your type. I see soldiers in the ER. Men who think their value is measured in how many bullets they can absorb. It's not noble. It's a death wish."

Something cracked behind his expression. Small, hairline.

"I'm not—" He stopped. His shadows went flat against the floor. "I've lost people before. People I was supposed to protect."

"When?"

"A long time ago."

I stood. "Three days. That's what you said—three days to find this rogue. Then I get to choose."

"Yes."

"Then for three days, I'm not your prisoner. I'm your partner. You teach me what I need to know. And when it's over, I walk away if I want to. No shadows following me. No compulsion. My choice."

"I can't compel you regardless."

"You know what I mean."

Kael studied me the way I studied bloodwork—looking for the thing that would change the diagnosis.

"You'll follow tactical instructions during any engagement."

"If they make sense, yes."

"They'll make sense. I've been doing this for centuries."

"And I've been keeping people alive for a decade. We both have relevant experience."

Something happened in his eyes. Not softening—more like the moment a locked door gives way. "Three days. I train you. We hunt Silas. When it's done, you choose."

"And if I choose to leave?"

His throat moved. A swallow. The shadows at his feet surged toward me, then pulled back as if corrected. "Then I let you go. One of the Council members will wipe your memory and you will forget about me, but I will remember you every moment of my eternal life."

He didn't believe he could let me leave. I could tell. And standing in his warehouse with his shadows whispering against my skin and the ruins of my old life glowing on a phone screen, I wasn't sure I believed it either.

"Deal."

He nodded once. Moved to a table near the door, strapped on weapons. "I need to hunt. The trail from the hospital is already cooling."

"Now? It's three AM."

"I'm a vampire, Maya. Three AM is Tuesday morning."

I blinked. "Did you just make a joke?"

"I made a statement. Vampires are nocturnal."

"That was a joke. You had timing and everything."

He pulled on a jacket, black as the rest of him. At the door, he paused. "The shadows will stay with you. They'll guard every entrance. If anything feels wrong—anything—they'll bring you to me."

"They can do that? Just... transport me?"

"They can do many things." He turned. The silver eyes found mine across the warehouse. "You're safer here than anywhere in this city. I need you to believe that."

"I believe you believe it."

"That'll do." He opened the door. Cold Minneapolis air knifed into the space. "There's a bed in the back room. Blankets in the cabinet. The kitchen—" He stopped. "I don't have food. I'll bring some."

"A vampire doing a grocery run. Sure. Why not."

The door closed behind him.

The shadows stayed.

They pooled around the door first, thick and dark, sealing the cracks. Then they spread—along the windowsills, under the frames, across the ceiling beams. A security system made of living darkness.

I stood in the middle of the warehouse and let myself shake.

Sixty seconds. I gave myself sixty seconds to fall apart. My hands trembled. My throat burned. My apartment was rubble and a vampire had claimed me as his fated mate and I was standing in his house surrounded by his sentient tattoo remnants.

I dried my face on my sleeve and started exploring.

The main space was exactly what it looked like—converted industrial. Open floor plan, high ceilings, minimal furniture. The leather couch. A low table with maps. The weapons rack. A desk with two monitors, both dark.

No photographs. No books. No personal effects. This wasn't a home. This was a forward operating base where someone happened to sleep.

I wandered into the back room. King-sized bed, plain gray sheets, military corners so tight I could bounce a quarter off them. A wooden cabinet held exactly four blankets, folded with precision.

Something nudged my ankle.

I looked down. A shadow—detached from the mass guarding the door, about the size of a house cat—had followed me. It pressed against my leg like a dog asking for attention.

"Hi."

It swirled. Tighter, faster. Happy?

"Can you understand me?"

The shadow stretched up my calf, wrapped around my knee, pulsed twice.

"Right. Cool. I'm talking to a shadow. This is my life now."

I sat on the edge of the bed. The shadow climbed into my lap—weightless, warm, impossible. Other shadows drifted in from the main room. They circled my feet, brushed my arms, one settled on my shoulder like a parrot made of smoke.

"He said you'd protect me."

The shadows pressed closer. The one on my shoulder curled against my neck, and something in my chest loosened.

My bangles caught the dim light as I lifted my hand. The shadows wrapped around them, threading between the gold like fingers lacing together.

"I lost her stuff tonight. Everything I had left." My voice came out smaller than I wanted. "A rogue vampire blew up my apartment and I lost her recipe cards and her photo and—"

The shadow on my shoulder tightened. Not squeezing. Holding.

I sat in bed, in a vampire's warehouse, wearing scrubs stained with blood, and let living shadows comfort me.

I pulled Kael's blanket around my shoulders. It smelled like leather and something dark. The shadows settled around me like a nest—door guarded, windows sealed, darkness watching.

I was sitting in the home of a man who'd lived for centuries and never once made it feel lived-in. A man whose magic had taken one look at me and decided I was worth wrapping around. A man who'd kidnapped me, yes, but who'd thrown his body over mine when the world exploded.

The warehouse was cold and empty and nothing like home.

I'd never felt safer in my life.

That was the most terrifying part.

3

First Touch

KAEL

The warehouse door didn't make a sound when I opened it. Silence was survival.

Tonight, silence let me hear her breathing from forty feet away.

Blood crusted my knuckles, cracking along the joints. Silas's thralls were scattered through the city like land mines—same dead yellow eyes, same programmed response: attack, flee, self-destruct. The third had given me a location that turned out to be empty. Recently empty.

He'd been there twenty minutes before me. Maybe less.

The shadows I'd left behind surged toward me—reporting. Every entrance sealed. No breaches. And—

She's in the bedroom. My bed.

Maya Reeves was asleep in my bed.

She looked like a small, stubborn storm caught in the middle of my bed, her long black hair finally freed from its practical bun and fanning out like black silk against my military-gray sheets. Even in the stillness of sleep, the exhausted dark circles beneath her eyes—the mark of a woman who had spent her life running on empty to save others—tugged at a part of me I thought had turned to stone centuries ago. She was South Asian, her rich brown skin a warm, vibrant contrast to the sterile, marble-pale of my own, and she looked as if she had been carved from something far more precious and fragile than I could ever hope to be.

She'd climbed under the covers, wrapped my blanket around herself like armor. Her hair fanned across my pillow, black silk against military gray. One arm stretched across the empty half of the mattress, palm up, fingers curled. Like she was reaching for something that wasn't there.

My shadows had abandoned their posts. Pooled around her instead. Under the covers, across the sheets, curled against her spine. They pulsed with her breathing, and the sensation was so foreign it took me three full seconds to identify it.

My shadows were content.

At five-foot-six and curvy, she was physically dwarfed by my frame, yet she possessed an 'ice-cold' presence that made her seem like the most dangerous thing in the room even while unconscious. I watched the way her fingers curled, her mother's gold bangles catching the low light. She was a hyper-competent trauma doctor whose world had just been reduced to rubble, yet her resilience made my three hundred years of survival feel suddenly, devastatingly hollow.

In that time no one had ever laid where she was lying. The bed was a place to recharge between missions. Four hours of unconsciousness, military efficient, no dreams.

She'd turned it into something else just by being in it.

Tear tracks had dried on her cheeks. She'd been crying. Grieving her apartment, her mother's things. And she'd chosen to be vulnerable here, in my most private space.

I should leave.

I didn't.

I lowered myself to the floor in the doorway. Leaned my back against the frame and watched her breathe.

The shadow at her throat pulsed. Warm. Protective.

Traitors.

She shifted. The blanket slipped off one shoulder. Her lips parted.

Her eyes opened.

MAYA

Silver.

Silver eyes, watching me from the doorway floor.

Kael sat with his back against the frame. Not lounging. Stationed. Like he'd assigned himself guard duty outside his own bedroom.

His knuckles were shredded.

Everything else vanished under medical reflex. Patient presents with bilateral metacarpophalangeal lacerations, slow-healing, active weeping.

I sat up. "How long have you been sitting there?"

"A while."

My feet hit cold concrete. Two steps and I was crouching in front of him, reaching for his hands. "Let me see."

His whole body locked as I turned his hand palm-up. The knuckles were split deep across all four ridges.

"These aren't healing properly."

"Silver rings. Slows the process."

"So vampire kryptonite is real. Great. Hold still."

My fingers traced the edge of one split, checking for embedded fragments—

His hand flinched.

Not from pain.

The shock traveled up my arm like a current. Every nerve ending in my fingers lit up where they pressed against his skin. My breath punched out.

His shadows erupted.

They exploded off every surface and converged on the point where my hand held his. Dark tendrils wrapped around our wrists, lacing our fingers together. The small shadow on my shoulder hummed—a vibration I felt in my sternum.

Kael yanked his hand free.

The shadows snapped back, and he was on his feet and across the room. Six feet of distance. Back pressed to the wall. Chest moving with breaths he didn't need.

"If I touch you now, I won't stop."

My hand hung in the air where his had been. The skin still tingled—no, more than tingled. Remembered.

"Kael."

"The Shadow Twin bond intensifies with contact. Skin to skin. Every touch makes the pull stronger. Right now I can resist it. Barely. If I touch you again—" He pressed his head back against the brick. "The bond creates a claiming instinct. Once I claim you, the connection becomes permanent. You need to understand what that means before—"

"Before what?"

His jaw worked. "Before I stop being able to give you a choice."

My pulse hammered a frantic, rebellious rhythm against that logic.

I stood. Took a step toward him. His shadows pressed flat against the wall.

"Maya."

Another step. "You said I'd have a choice."

"You do. Right now. If you walk back to that bed, the pull settles. We can function. Work together." His voice dropped. "If you come closer, I can't—I won't—"

"You won't stop."

"No."

One more step. Close enough to feel the cold radiating off his skin. His eyes burned silver-white and his hands pressed flat against the brick like he was trying to push himself through the wall.

Years of control, of empty beds and solitary missions and never letting himself want something for himself. And now he stood shaking, terrified of what he'd do when I got there.

I knew that terror. Control was my religion. Because the one time I'd let go, someone died.

"Maybe I don't want you to stop."

His eyes searched my face. Looking for hesitation. For any sign that the bond was making this choice instead of me.

"I'm not the bond," I said. "I'm a thirty-year-old doctor with terrible taste in timing and a track record of making life decisions at three AM. And I'm telling you—" I lifted my hand, let it hover an inch from his chest. "I want this. Not the magic. Not the fate. You."

His hand closed around mine.

The world shifted.

His shadows surged off the wall and wrapped around both of us. His skin against mine sent that current racing again, and this time neither of us pulled away.

He kissed me.

Not gentle. Not tentative. I grabbed the front of his jacket and held on. His palms found my face, cupped it, angled me closer. Cold fingers against my jaw, threading into my hair. I tasted copper and something darker—old rain, winter roads, a life spent moving through darkness.

His arms locked around me, lifting me effortlessly. The world narrowed to the heat of his mouth, the solid strength of his body, the way his shadows cleared the path to the bed.

He laid me down on sheets still warm from my body. His eyes burned silver in the dim light.

"You're sure."

I arched a brow. "If you ask me that one more time, I'm billing you for the consultation."

A crack split his granite facade—not quite a smile, but close.

He stripped off his weapons with methodical precision. Shoulder holster, knives. Each one placed on the night-stand with the care of a ritual. The jacket followed. Beneath it, a black shirt streaked with dried blood.

I sat up and tugged at the hem. He froze.

"I've seen blood before," I said. "Get down here."

He let me pull the shirt over his head.

The shadow tattoos writhed across his skin—moving like living things. Dark lines coiled and branched, revealing muscle honed by centuries of violence. A single scar cut across his left ribs, old and white. The shadows avoided it, flowing around it like water around stone.

I traced the scar with my fingertips. His abs tensed.

"What did this?"

"Enchanted blade. Three hundred years ago. Protecting someone."

"Did they live?"

A pause. The shadows flattened. "No."

I pressed my lips to the scar. His hand found the back of my head, fingers tangling in my hair, and the sound he made—low, broken, raw—wasn't one I'd ever heard.

"Maya—"

"I know." I pulled back just enough to meet his eyes. "I know I've known you for less than eight hours and this is clinically insane."

"It is insane."

"And I don't care." I cupped his face. "I'm choosing this."

He came down over me, shadows pooling beneath us, sealing us in a cocoon of warm darkness. Just his mouth on my collarbone, his hands on my skin.

He peeled the scrubs off me with agonizing slowness, kissing every inch of skin he revealed. His lips were cold at first, then warmed against me. The shadows followed, tracing every place he'd touched. *Sentient tattoo-tentacles. My therapist is going to need a raise.*

"Does it always feel like this?"

His mouth paused against my hip. "I don't know. I've never had this."

I reached for him. He caught my wrist, stared at the gold bangles against my brown skin and his pale fingers.

"These were your mother's."

"Yes."

He pressed his lips to the bangles, then to the inside of my wrist, then to my palm. Each touch sent a current through me, and the shadows responded—binding wrist to wrist, pulling us closer.

I'd expected cold. Vampire, undead, shadow creature.

The data was very wrong.

He burned everywhere he touched me—not with heat, but with intensity. His hands knew the human body, and every place they landed left me gasping, arching, pulling him closer. The shadows wove between us—against my thighs, my wrists, the small of my back—and the sensation was indescribable. Something that made me laugh and moan in the same breath.

"That's—those are your—"

"Shadows. They're part of me." His forehead dropped against mine. Our breath mingled. "You feel them."

"I feel everything."

His hands slid down my body until his fingers found the heat between my legs. I gasped as he teased me, his touch expert, relentless. The shadows wrapped around my wrists, my ankles, pulling me open for him.

"Kael—"

"Let me," he growled. "Let me give you this."

His thumb circled my clit, his fingers curling inside me, and the shadows tightened as pleasure coiled tighter.

"Oh god—"

"Not god. Just me."

I came with a cry, the shadows pulsing around me in time with my release. His mouth found mine again, swallowing my moans as aftershocks rippled through me.

When I finally came down, I pushed him onto his back, straddling his hips. His erection pressed against me, hard and insistent, and I grinned.

"My turn."

I slid down his body until I reached the waistband of his pants. I freed him, my breath catching. He was thick, hard, and the shadows coiled around him like they couldn't bear to be apart.

I wrapped my hand around him before leaning down and taking him into my mouth.

His hips jerked, a groan tearing from his throat. "Maya—fuck—"

I hummed around him, the vibration making him shudder. His hands tangled in my hair as I took him deeper. His shadows wrapped around my wrists, and I could feel his control slipping with every stroke.

"Maya, I—" His voice was rough, desperate. "I haven't—it's been—"

I pulled back just enough to grin up at him.

And then I took him deep again, and his control shattered. His hips bucked, and he came with a growl, his release spilling down my throat. I swallowed every drop before pulling back.

He pulled me up, crushing his mouth to mine, his hands roaming my body like he couldn't get enough. When he finally broke the kiss, his forehead rested against mine.

"I should mark you," he said, his voice rough. "Not just the bite. I'll give you my blood. It'll protect you. Heal you faster. Connect us—not permanently, but it's the start."

I pressed my fingers to his lips. "Yes."

His eyes flashed silver. "You're sure?"

"I'm sure."

"The mark makes you mine in every way that matters to vampire law."

"Will it hurt?"

"Yes. And then it won't."

I turned my head, "Do it."

His fangs grazed my skin—a scrape, a test.

Then he bit down.

The pain was sharp, clean, precise. A sound tore out of me—half-cry, half-his-name. The shadows exploded around us, and in the space between heartbeats, the pain transformed into something else entirely.

I felt him. Not near me—in me. His presence, his emotions, his loneliness crashing into my grief. His relief. His terror. His wonder that someone was here, choosing him, staying.

His hand moved, and through the haze I heard a sharp sound—blade across palm.

His hand appeared in front of me, blood welling dark in the cut. "Drink," he murmured. "Just a little. It'll connect us, help you heal faster."

The cut was already closing. I had maybe seconds.

I caught his wrist, pressed my mouth to his palm, and tasted him.

Copper and night and something wild.

The shadows went nova. His grip on me tightened, and the bond between us flared bright enough I gasped.

When I could breathe again, his forehead was pressed to my shoulder, his whole body trembling. "Maya," he whispered. Just my name. Like a prayer.

"Mine," he growled.

"Yours," I agreed.

His thumb traced the mark on my shoulder. Two small punctures, already closing, surrounded by a shadow-dark bruise that pulsed with faint light.

He rolled us until I was tucked against his chest, his arms locked around me, shadows settling over us like a second blanket. No heartbeat beneath my ear. Just silence and the steady rise and fall of breaths he chose to take.

"Kael?"

"Mm."

"I haven't felt safe since my mother died." The words came out without permission. "Two years. Every room I walk into, I check the exits. Every patient I lose, I carry home. Every night I come back to an empty apartment because at least if I'm alone, nobody else can—"

His arms tightened.

"—nobody else can leave. And then you showed up, and I fell asleep in your bed, and—" My throat closed. I forced it open. "And it was the first time in two years I didn't check the exits."

He said nothing. Held me. The shadows pressed in—warm, steady, present.

"I feel safe with you. Safer than I've felt since she died. And that terrifies me."

His lips found my hairline. Pressed there. Stayed.

"You terrify me too." The words rumbled through his chest. "You're the most frightening thing I've ever encountered."

"That's—I can't tell if that's romantic or insulting."

"Both." His hand spread across my lower back. "It's both."

We lay in the dark. Breathing. Existing. The mark on my shoulder throbbed with a pulse that wasn't mine—his rhythm, syncing with my body.

His phone buzzed on the nightstand.

Then again. Three times in quick succession.

Kael's arm reached over me. The screen lit his face in blue-white.

I watched his expression harden. Every trace of the man who'd just pressed his lips to my hair sealed itself behind stone. The Sentinel returned in the space of a single breath.

"What is it?"

He turned the screen toward me.

Three messages from THERON:

Silas knows about her.

He's coming for her.

Lock down. NOW.

4

Lockdown

MAYA

Three texts. That's all it took to turn a fortress into a cage.

I was out of bed, pulling on Kael's t-shirt and my discarded pants while he armed himself—shoulder holster, knives at hip, back, ankle. He dressed for war in the time it took me to zip my fly.

"Talk to me."

He was already dialing. "Silas has your name. Your address. He burned your apartment two hours ago."

Well, at least I don't have to water the plant anymore.

He read my face, shadows flattening against his skin. "Raj is safe. That's what matters."

"What matters is that you don't get to unilaterally decide—"

He held up one finger. Someone had answered.

I wanted to break that finger.

"Theron. She's awake. I need Draven." Pause. His expression tightened. "How many thralls?" Another pause. "Understood. Twenty minutes."

He disconnected. "Silas is accelerating. Three more corrupted thralls found in six hours, all targeting hospital witnesses. Your coworkers are being moved. Draven is coming to reinforce the wards. Your brother will be here within the hour."

"Brought here by who?"

"Sentinels."

I headed for the bathroom. "I'm going to brush my teeth with my finger and then we're going to have a very loud conversation about boundaries."

"I don't have any toothpaste."

"Of course you don't. You've been alive forever and own zero dental hygiene products."

I shut the door. Leaned against it and breathed.

My apartment was gone. My job compromised. My brother being escorted by vampires to a warehouse where I was hiding with my—what? Three-hundred-year-old shadow-wielding kidnapper I'd made out with six hours after meeting him?

The claiming mark on my shoulder throbbed. Two small puncture marks surrounded by a faintly glowing bruise. Kael's rhythm, synced into my skin.

I'd chosen this. The question was whether choosing also meant surrendering every decision to a man who thought protection meant making choices for me.

I walked back out ready for a fight.

I didn't get one. Because the far wall was opening.

Stone and brick separated like a curtain, edges glowing emerald. A man stepped through the gap like it was a doorway he used every Tuesday.

Okay. So walls are optional now. Great.

Tall. Broad-shouldered. Dark brown hair falling past his ears—forgotten, not neglected. Brown leather jacket, dark clothes. Everything about him suggested earth tones and heavy gravity.

Then his eyes landed on me.

Emerald. Not green—emerald. The color of the light in the walls, concentrated and burning in irises that didn't look entirely human.

Three seconds. Four. Five.

Kael's shadows reared up. "Stop staring at my mate, Draven."

The man blinked. His gaze dropped. Anywhere but me.

"Apologies." His voice came out rough. Unused. "Haven't seen a Shadow Twin bond in person. It's... rare."

Pain. That word came wrapped in something that hurt to hear.

"Draven Emeris. Blood Architect. He's here to reinforce the wards."

"Blood Architect means...?"

Draven pressed one palm against the wall. His eyes blazed. Light traced through the mortar in branching patterns—capillary networks, my brain supplied. The light spread, climbed, crossed the ceiling. The entire building hummed.

"Means that," Kael said.

Draven moved methodically along the wall, both hands working. His face had gone blank. Relieved. Like touching stone was easier than touching air in a room with people.

"He seems lonely," I murmured.

"Nine centuries alone. Says he prefers it."

I watched him press his hands against brick like it was the only thing holding him together. "That's the biggest lie I've heard all day, and I woke up in a vampire's bed."

"I know." Kael's shadows curled around my wrist. "Not everyone finds what they're looking for."

Draven finished in twelve minutes. The walls now pulsed with emerald lattice. He walked back toward his entrance.

"The wards will hold against anything short of a House-level assault."

"Thank you."

"I'm Maya, by the way. Thanks for fortifying my prison."

He stopped. Turned his head just enough that I caught his profile. "It's a safe house. Not a prison."

"Depends which side of the wall you're standing on."

The smallest twitch at the corner of his mouth. Then the stone closed behind him.

"He does that," Kael said. "Arrives. Works. Leaves. I've known him eighty years. He's said maybe four hundred words to me total."

"That's five words a year."

"He's efficient."

I turned to face him. Crossed my arms. "Now that your stone wizard is done bricking me in, let's talk about the part where you sent vampires after my brother without asking me."

"It was the right call."

"It was *a* call. One that wasn't yours to make alone."

"He would have been dead by morning if I'd waited."

"You don't know that."

"I do. Silas eliminates vulnerabilities. Your brother is your vulnerability. The math was simple."

"My brother is not *math*."

The shadows on his arms went flat. This was Kael shutting down.

"You want to talk about what this is actually about?" I stepped toward him. "This isn't about Raj. This is about you making decisions for me. About me sitting here like a package to be protected while you go out there and—"

"And what?"

"And die for me."

Silence.

"That's the plan, isn't it? You go hunt Silas. If it goes wrong, you throw yourself between me and whatever comes through that door. You've already made peace with that."

His jaw worked. Silver eyes burning.

He cupped my face. "I think keeping you alive is the only thing that matters. That is our Shadow Twin bond. It's the most precious connection. It brings great happiness to a long eternal life." His thumb traced my cheekbone, shadows curling toward me. "I want that. But I want you safe more than I want anything in this world."

Two people standing in a fortified warehouse, both built from grief and control and the absolute refusal to let anyone else carry the weight.

"Teach me to fight."

"No."

"Teach me to fight, or I walk out that door the second you leave and find Silas myself."

"The wards would stop you."

"Want to bet?"

He moved to the center of the warehouse. Pulled a training pad from a gear rack. "Vampire combat isn't about strength. It's about positioning. Speed. Knowing where teeth and claws are going before they get there. Hit this."

I hit it.

"No. You're punching from your shoulder. Power comes from your hips. Rotate."

I rotated. Hit again. Better.

"Again."

Twelve times. Twenty. He adjusted my stance—cold hands on my waist, my elbow, the turn of my foot. Every correction precise. And under it—the current. Running between us where skin met skin.

"If a vampire grabs you, don't pull away. Push in. Their leverage fails at close range."

I pushed. Stumbled. Tried again. Got it.

"If fangs come for your throat—chin down. Protect the artery. Give them the shoulder."

"Got it. Offer them the less-juicy parts."

I drilled the movement until it lived in my muscles. His shadows crept across the floor and wound around my ankles. Not restraining. Steadying.

The warehouse door banged open.

I spun into a fighting stance and Kael materialized between me and the entrance.

Two figures in tactical gear. Between them, a twenty-two-year-old in a University of Minnesota hoodie with terror on his face.

"Maya?"

"Raj."

I went around Kael, around the shadows trying to hold me back. My arms wrapped around my brother.

"What the hell is happening? Two guys showed up at my dorm—"

"I know. I'm sorry." I pulled back. Checked his pupils, his color, his pulse. "You're okay. You're not hurt."

"I'm not hurt, I'm confused." His eyes moved past me. To Kael. To the shadows and weapons and silver eyes fixed on him with predatory assessment.

Raj straightened. Stepped partially in front of me. All five-foot-eleven, one-hundred-sixty-pounds of pre-law student positioning himself between his sister and a vampire.

I loved him so much my chest hurt.

"So. What are you?"

"A Shadow Sentinel for House Adamas. And a vampire."

Raj's expression cycled through disbelief, shock, landed on acceptance. "Vampires are real."

"Yes."

"And you..." He gestured at me. "What's she to you?"

"My Shadow Twin. A fated bond. One person in the world who's compatible. On every level."

"Soulmates."

"Essentially."

"And you kidnapped her."

"I saved her life. There's a rogue vampire hunting witnesses. Maya's a target."

"She's wearing your clothes."

Kael's shadows flickered.

"We need to talk." Raj dropped his backpack. "Outside. Now."

"I don't go outside during daylight."

"Then in the corner. Away from my sister."

"Raj—"

"Five minutes, Maya." He shot me the look. Mom's look. "Five minutes."

I watched my baby brother walk Kael Nightshade into a corner. Watched Raj point at his chest and start talking. Watched Kael stand there and take it.

Four minutes later, Raj walked back. "He cares about you."

"How can you tell?"

"He let me yell at him. I called him seven different names and he just stood there. No one takes that from a college kid unless they're trying to pass inspection."

Kael returned. His shadows brushed my wrist. Are you okay?

I pressed my fingers against them. *Yes.*

Raj sat on the couch and pulled out his phone. "So vampires are real. Thralls are a thing. My sister is mated to a shadow warrior. Is there a FAQ, or...?"

The warehouse door opened again. Slow. One of the Sentinels stepped inside, face white.

"Sir. There's something at the door."

We followed him. The thrall lay on the doorstep like a package.

Dead. Female, mid-twenties, blonde hair matted with blood. Yellow-tinged eyes staring at nothing.

A note was pinned to her jacket. Through fabric and skin.

Turn over the girl. Midnight. Japanese Garden, Como Park.

Or I visit the brother next.

Kael's shadows detonated.

They ripped off his skin in a black surge that filled the space—a living darkness that threw itself around me and Raj, pressing us back. Protective. Primal.

The emerald lattice flared. Draven's wards pushing back.

"Kael." I pushed through the shadows. They parted for me—only me. "Kael. Look at me."

Silver eyes. No pupil. Pure light, burning in a face I barely recognized.

I put my hand on his chest. Over the silence where his heart should be.

"We have until midnight. Eighteen hours. We plan. We prepare. We fight."

The shadows trembled. Pulled in. Settled—contained. Focused.

"Together," I said.

His hand covered mine. Cold fingers gripping too hard.

"Together."

Behind us, Raj looked at the dead girl, then at me, then at the vampire whose shadows wrapped around his sister like living armor.

He picked up his phone and started typing.

"What are you doing?"

"Googling 'vampire brother-in-law etiquette.' I'm assuming there's a Reddit thread for this."

5

Vulnerability

KAEL

"We need to talk about tonight."

Maya's voice cut through my preparation. I kept my back to her, sliding a magazine into my vest. Silver stakes, three; throwing daggers, four.

"The plan is simple," I said. "I go to Como Park. I draw Silas out. I end this."

"I'm sorry—you go?"

"Alone."

She moved between me and the weapons rack, barefoot, wearing my shirt. The claiming mark glowed faint gold at her collarbone.

"No."

"He wants you, Maya. You walk into that park, you're giving him everything."

"And you walking in alone is—what? A better plan?"

"I've fought worse odds." My jaw locked. "I'm a Sentinel. This is what I do."

"Die for people?" She stepped closer. "That's the job description? Three centuries of finding people to die for?"

"We're partners or nothing." Her chin came up. "You said together."

"That was before he threatened your brother."

From the couch: "I'm right here, by the way."

We both ignored Raj.

"He'll kill you to hurt me." My voice went clinical. "You walk into that park, you become leverage."

"And if you go alone and he kills you, what am I supposed to do? Sit here and wait until your shadows stop moving and I know—"

Her voice cracked. Not anger. Fear.

"I can't sit here and lose someone else. Not you. Not like—" She stopped. "Not like my mother."

The warehouse went quiet. Even my shadows stilled.

"You both are going to get yourselves killed," Raj said. "You fight together or you die separately. Pick one."

Maya looked at me. I looked at her.

She turned and walked toward the fire escape.

My shadows strained after her. I made it fourteen seconds before I followed.

The roof was freezing. She sat on the ledge, feet hanging five stories over the alley, wind cutting through my shirt. I climbed over and stood three feet away.

"You're going to fall," I said.

"You'd catch me."

"Yes."

We watched the sun bleed down behind the skyline.

"Why does dying for me feel like a plan to you?"

I was quiet for a long time. Long enough that streetlights blinked on and the sky shifted to bruised purple.

"In 1847, I was stationed outside a farmhouse in Ohio."

She turned her head. I kept my eyes on the skyline.

"There was a family. Two parents, three children. The youngest was four." My voice stripped down. "A rogue had claimed the territory. Theron sent me to protect them until extraction."

"I left for six hours. Standard reconnaissance. I told them to stay inside. Lock the doors."

My shadows curled inward.

"The rogue came through the root cellar. I hadn't checked the root cellar."

"I found them at dawn. All five. The children were still in their nightclothes."

"Kael—"

"I've checked every cellar since. Every crawl space, every attic. Three hundred years of checking." I looked at my hands. "It doesn't bring them back."

"You think if you die protecting me, it fixes Ohio."

"I think I've failed before," I said. "I think the people I'm supposed to protect end up dead. I think you're the most important person I've ever been asked to keep alive, and the pattern says I'm going to lose you too."

"So you go first. You die before I can."

"Yes."

"That's not protection, Kael. That's punishment."

Her eyes were raw. She saw all of it.

"You're punishing yourself. You've been punishing yourself for years, and now you've found someone you love and your brain says great, here's a new way to suffer."

"You don't understand—"

"I do." Her throat tightened. "My mother was an ER doctor. Same hospital. Same shift I work now."

I went still.

"Two years ago she left after a double shift. A man with a knife wanted her wallet." She stared at her bangles. "She was a trauma specialist. She knew how to survive until help came."

"The stab wound hit her femoral artery. She would have known exactly how long she had." Her fingers closed around the bangles. "I was in the hospital. Three floors up. I would have heard the code if I'd been paying attention. But I was *charting*."

"Maya."

"I became her. Same hospital, same specialty, same shift. I work until I can't see straight and I tell myself it's honoring her legacy, but it's not." The truth peeled out. "It's penance. I wasn't there when she needed me, so now I'm there for everyone. I never go home and I never sleep and I never stop because if I stop—"

Her voice broke.

"If you stop, you have to feel it," I said.

She nodded.

I sat beside her. My thigh against hers. My shadows crawled from my arms to hers—a blanket made of night.

"You're surviving," I said. "Not living."

"So are you."

She wiped her eyes and my shadow curled around her wrist.

"We're the same," she said. "Two broken people who found each other and immediately started arguing about who gets to die first."

"When you say it like that—"

"It sounds insane? Yeah. Welcome to my inner monologue. Population: one panicking doctor who's somehow bonded to a vampire with a martyr complex."

My mouth almost smiled.

"I'm scared," she said. "Not of Silas. Of you going somewhere I can't follow."

My hand found hers. Cold fingers lacing through warm ones.

"I'm scared too." The admission cost me. "I've never had something to lose before. Not like this."

"Together," she said. "We go together or we don't go at all."

"*Together.*"

"Say it like you mean it."

"Together." My shadows surged—up her arms, around her shoulders, wrapping her in darkness that felt like a promise.

She kissed me.

MAYA

His mouth was cold. Mine was not.

We met somewhere in the middle—a temperature that could only happen when a dead man and a living woman stopped running from each other.

He tasted like shadows and grief and something underneath that was just him. His hand cupped my neck. My fingers grabbed his vest and pulled.

"Inside," I breathed.

His shadows carried us through the fire escape, and then we were in the warehouse and Raj was on the couch and—

"Going to bed," I said without stopping.

Raj looked up. "It's six thirty PM."

"Goodnight, Raj."

"I'm going to need so much therapy." He put his earbuds in and turned away.

The bedroom door closed. Kael's hands found my waist.

"We don't have to—"

"If we die tonight, I want this. I want you. All of you."

His silver eyes burned. Something that had been locked away.

He pulled his shirt off me. Slow. The claiming mark flared gold and his fingers traced it—reverent, disbelieving, afraid.

"You're real," he said.

"I'm real."

"Kael." I took his face in my hands. "I'm real. I'm here. And I'm not going anywhere without you."

His shadows stripped the room of everything that wasn't us.

He laid me down and covered me with his body and the dark.

Shadows slid along my arms, pinning my wrists above my head—not restraining. Anchoring. I arched and his breath hitched.

"Tell me if—"

"Don't stop."

"I will tell you. Now stop talking and touch me."

He touched me.

Hands mapped the places that made me gasp. Everywhere his fingers went, shadows followed—tracing patterns that felt like being written on. Claimed.

I pulled at his vest. The buckles gave and then there was nothing between us—his chest against mine, shadow tattoos writhing where our skin met, the bond humming in my teeth.

"I can feel you," he said against my throat. "Through the bond. Everything you're feeling."

"Good." I dragged my nails down his back. "Feel this."

He groaned, and his shadows tightened, and my spine curved off the bed.

We moved together. Raw. Unpolished. Two people crashing into each other.

His mouth found the claiming mark and the bond sang. I felt his fear. His love. His certainty that I was worth more than his survival, and his certainty that he was not worth mine.

I grabbed his face and pulled him up.

"You are worth this," I said. "You are worth living for. Not dying for. Living."

His silver eyes went bright. Wet.

"Say it back to me."

"I—"

"Say it."

"I love you." The words ripped out. "I love you and it terrifies me."

"I love you." I pulled him closer. Wrapped my legs around him. "I love you and it terrifies me too."

We said it at the same time and laughed—breathless, shaking—and then he moved inside me and the laughter became something else. Something that spread through every nerve, every shadow, every inch of the bond.

His shadows wound around us both. Binding. Every point of contact deepened. I felt what he felt—my warmth, the ache in his chest that was three centuries of loneliness dissolving. He felt what I felt—the terror and joy and fierce certainty that this man was mine.

He pressed his forehead to mine. The shadows pulsed around us, a heartbeat that belonged to neither of us and both.

"I want to bite you," he said. Strained.

"Then do it."

"No." He pulled back. "Not before a fight. If I feed and something happens to you, the bond backlash—" He stopped. "I need to be sharp tonight."

"After, then."

"After." He kissed me. "When we're safe. When I can take my time."

"Is that a promise?"

"That's a guarantee."

We lay tangled afterward. My head on his chest—no heartbeat, just the solid presence of him.

"If I die tonight," I said, "would you convert me?"

His body went rigid.

"Tell me the truth."

He was quiet. "Conversion requires complete draining. Your heart stops. You die. Not metaphorically. You die."

I absorbed that. The doctor in me cataloged the process. "Then what?"

"My blood carries the virus. If I feed it to you before draining, it activates when your body shuts down. It rebuilds you. Rewrites your cells. You come back different."

"How different?"

"Immortal. Faster, stronger. Frozen at peak condition." His fingers traced my shoulder. "The transformation takes two to three days. Pain like nothing you've experienced."

"That's... horrifying."

"Yes."

"Have you done it before?"

"No." His shadows pressed against my skin. "Every vampire gets one conversion. It's meant for your Shadow Twin. I had not found mine."

"Until now."

"Until you."

I lay there processing. The doctor brain ran the scenario—blood loss, cellular reconstruction, three days of agony.

"If it comes to that," I said. "If I'm dying and there's no other way. Do it."

"Maya—"

"I'm choosing this. I'm choosing you. All of you, including the terrifying immortal virus part." I propped up on one elbow. "But let's make sure it doesn't come to that. Let's make a plan that keeps us both alive."

His hand covered mine.

"Okay," he said. "Here's the plan."

Ten PM. Two hours until midnight.

Kael moved through the warehouse checking weapons, testing comm equipment, coordinating with Theron.

Raj sat at the table with his laptop. "So the thralls are basically on a remote frequency. Silas's blood corruption acts like a signal. If we disrupt it—"

"You want to jam vampire blood magic with technology?"

"I want to create a distraction. Electromagnetic interference won't break the bond, but it'll confuse their systems. Hit them with enough sensory overload and they'll hesitate. Maybe two seconds."

"Two seconds is enough." Kael appeared beside the table, fully armed. "Where do you place the devices?"

"Japanese garden. Four entry points. I can rig portable EMP bursts—I need forty minutes and three hundred dollars."

"Done." Kael pulled out cash. "Take the south exit. One of my Sentinels will drive you."

Raj grabbed the money. Paused. Looked at me.

"Don't die."

"Don't blow yourself up."

"No promises." He hugged me, then was gone.

Kael turned to me.

"You're the bait."

"I know."

"He'll try to separate you from me. Don't let him."

He reached into the weapons rack and pulled out a silver knife. Placed it in my palm.

"Silver burns vampires. You don't need to kill him. You need to make him let go long enough for me to get there."

I tested the weight.

"One more thing." He took my left wrist. His shadows crept across my skin, winding around my mother's bangles, threading through the gold. The shadow solidified—a cuff of living darkness locked alongside the gold.

"My shadows will stay with you. Even when I'm not close. They'll protect you."

I touched the shadow bracelet. It pulsed. Warm. Alive.

"They'll know? If something's coming?"

"Before you do. Trust them."

I looked at him. Full tactical gear, silver eyes bright with lethal focus. Shadow Sentinel. Three centuries of violence refined into a weapon.

And underneath—the man on the roof who'd said I love you like a confession held for lifetimes.

"Ready?"

"No." I slid the knife into my belt. Felt the shadow bracelet pulse. "Let's go anyway."

His hand found mine. Cold fingers, warm grip. We walked toward the warehouse door together.

6
The Trap

Maya

Como Park at 11:45 PM looked like an innocent winter wonderland. Snow on the trees, moonlight on ice. The kind of quiet that would be peaceful if I wasn't here to be vampire bait.

Kael killed the engine two blocks from the garden. The Sentinels were positioned, Draven was south, and Raj was on the hill with his laptop, three EMP devices, and what I assumed was a stress-induced energy drink problem.

My family, ladies and gentlemen. A vampire hit squad and a college kid with homemade electromagnetic bombs.

"Fifteen minutes." Kael's voice, low in the dark.

"I can tell time."

His hand found mine. The shadow bracelet pulsed at my wrist—steady, rhythmic.

"The Sentinels have north and west. Draven has south. I'll be thirty feet away—"

"I know the plan, Kael."

"I'm telling myself the plan."

Silver eyes glowing in the dark. Full tactical gear. Three centuries of violence coiled behind the face of a man who'd told me he loved me four hours ago.

"You're scared," I said.

"Terrified."

"Good. Scared people don't do anything stupid."

"That is categorically untrue."

I squeezed his hand. His shadows crept up my arm, wrapping past the bracelet, clinging.

"They're worried about me."

"They're not the only ones."

He cupped my face, forehead touching mine. "Come back to me."

"I will."

He kissed me—brief, fierce—then dissolved into shadow.

I sat alone for ten seconds. Touched the silver knife at my belt, the shadow bracelet at my wrist.

"Okay, Mom," I said to no one. "Your daughter is about to be vampire bait. Bet you didn't see that coming."

The walk took four minutes. Snow crunched under borrowed combat boots two sizes too big. Every step sounded like a gunshot.

Through the bond, I felt Kael. His fear, sharp and metallic. His focus. His pride.

The stone torii gate marked the garden entrance. I stopped.

11:58 PM.

The garden spread before me: stone lanterns, frozen pond, sculpted pines. Peaceful. Meditative.

Of course the genocidal maniac wants to meet in a meditation garden.

I walked to the center of the bridge—highest ground, maximum exposure. If I was bait, I'd be good bait.

Midnight.

Nothing.

One minute. Two. Three.

"You're braver than I expected."

The voice came from everywhere. Smooth. Conversational.

I turned.

Silas Mordain stepped from behind a stone lantern. Charcoal suit, cashmere overcoat, leather shoes in six inches of snow. He looked like a hedge fund manager.

Second impression: *wrong*.

His smile was too wide. His eyes caught moonlight and threw it back yellow. His movements twitched, like video at 1.1x speed.

My lizard brain was screaming at me to run.

"Dr. Reeves. Or do you prefer Maya?"

"I prefer Doctor."

"Professional to the end." He circled left. "Do you know why I asked to meet you here?"

"Flair for the dramatic?"

"Japanese gardens encourage calm decisions."

"What decision?"

"Give me what I want and walk away alive."

The shadow bracelet burned. Kael's fear spiked through the bond.

"You blew up my hospital," I said flatly. "People died."

"Collateral damage. The thrall was a prototype."

"That's what you call a human you turned into a puppet?"

"Progress." He studied me. "Do you know what a thrall army can do?"

I didn't care about his answer. I cared about buying time for the Sentinels to position, for Raj's EMPs to charge.

"Vampires have a limitation," Silas said. "One conversion per lifetime. The Council's rule." He held up a finger. "But thralls are unlimited. Corrupt the bond, remove free will, and suddenly you have soldiers who don't question."

"They also die. The corruption is toxic."

"They last long enough."

"For what?"

"A coup. The Houses have controlled vampire society for millennia. Stagnant old blood. The Council dictates everything." His yellow eyes burned. "I'm going to change that."

Thrall army. Coup attempt.

"That doesn't explain why you need me dead."

"I don't need you dead." Too many teeth in that smile. "I need what's bonded to you."

The shadow bracelet went ice-cold.

"Your mate. A Shadow Sentinel. Three centuries of combat experience, shadow magic powerful enough to breach Council defenses. Bound to a mortal woman he'd do anything to protect." He stepped closer. "A leash."

My throat tightened with rage.

"You want to use me to control him."

"Threaten a Shadow Twin and the strongest vampire becomes the weakest. Emotion overrides training."

He extended a hand. "Give him to me. Walk away. One mortal woman for the tools I need."

I looked at his hand. Manicured nails, no calluses. A hand that had never held a scalpel, never fought to keep a heartbeat going.

"Not a chance."

His smile shifted. The charm drained out, replaced by something cold and hungry.

"Wrong answer, Doctor."

He snapped his fingers.

They came from the treeline.

Six corrupted thralls. Yellow eyes glowing. No expression. Puppet precision.

Two seconds of terror.

Then Raj's EMP devices detonated—silent pressure waves that made my fillings ache and stopped the thralls mid-stride.

They froze. Twitched. Yellow eyes flickering.

Kael materialized behind the nearest thrall, shadows erupting. The thrall dropped.

The Sentinels hit from north and west. Four figures of shadow, vampire-fast, crashing into the thrall line.

The stone path split open.

Draven Emeris rose from the earth, brushing granite dust from his shoulders. Green eyes burning.

He pressed both palms to the ground.

Stone barriers punched upward, cutting off escape routes, funneling the fight into kill zones.

I watched him fight. No wasted energy. Every movement surgical. He redirected a thrall into a wall, turned ground to quicksand beneath two others. The Sentinels gave him wide berth. He fought like he was utterly alone, and had been for a very long time.

A hand grabbed my arm.

Yellow eyes. Blank face. Thrall.

Training kicked in. I twisted into the grip, gained space, drove the silver knife into its forearm.

The blade sank deep. Burning flesh, smoke. The grip loosened—mechanical failure.

I ripped free.

Second thrall from my left, moving fast—

Draven intercepted at full speed. One hand on its face, the other on its chest. The thrall flew backward into stone.

He turned to me. Green eyes assessing. For two seconds something passed through his expression—the look of someone on the wrong side of a window.

Then his hand was on my elbow, steering me, and Kael was there with blood on his knuckles.

Draven placed my arm in Kael's grip. Dropped his hand. Turned back to the fight.

"Are you hurt?" Kael's hands checked me.

"I'm fine."

"Your knife?"

"In a thrall's arm."

"That's my girl."

Three thralls down. Two in shadow restraints. One crawling with a broken spine.

Silas.

I scanned the garden. And saw him—behind Kael. Fifteen feet back, moving fast from the east end where no one had positioned defenses.

Claws extended. Black, curved, dripping with venom.

Aimed at Kael's spine.

The bond screamed.

I moved.

My body hit Kael's side, shoved him left. The claws meant for his spine found my right shoulder instead.

They went deep.

Pressure and cold and the sound of muscle separating from bone.

Then the venom.

Frozen fire spreading from the wound—through my shoulder, down my arm, across my chest. My legs buckled. White ground, red blood.

Silas's claws pulled free.

I hit the ground.

The snow was soft. My blood melted through to frozen earth beneath.

The shadow bracelet pulsed—a scream of panic that wasn't mine.

Kael's face appeared above me. Silver eyes blown wide. Shadows erupting from his skin, snapping and writhing.

"Maya. Maya."

I tasted copper.

The venom spread. My fingers went numb.

"I'm okay," I tried to say. The words came out slurred, distant.

I wasn't okay.

The cold kept spreading.

7
Feral

Kael

Her pain hit me through the bond like a blade between the ribs. Maya's blood on the snow—arterial spray, deep wound, fast bleed. The venom spreading through her shoulder, cold and toxic, and I felt every inch of it as if Silas had driven his claws into my own body.

Something inside my chest snapped. A wire held taut for three hundred and forty-seven years.

My shadows exploded outward in a wall of living darkness that swallowed the garden.

Threat. Silas standing over her with red on his claws.

Eliminate.

I stopped thinking.

I don't remember crossing the distance. One second watching her blood melt through snow. The next my hands were tearing through the nearest thrall like paper. Bones snapped. A body hit the stone barrier with a wet crunch.

My shadows caught another thrall, squeezed. It dropped.

Three centuries of discipline—gone. Replaced by something ancient with one function: protect what's mine.

Silas ran. Too late.

He shadow-traveled toward the treeline. I tracked him through every shadow in this garden. My territory. My darkness.

My shadows hooked his ankle, his throat, yanked him from the dark passage and slammed him into frozen ground hard enough to crack earth.

I was on him. Knees pinning his arms. Hands on his throat. Squeezing.

Kill him.

My claws extended.

Maya's heartbeat stuttered through the bond. Weak. Irregular. Dying.

Silas laughed through my grip. "Choose. Kill me—or watch her die."

I looked at him. Yellow eyes. Her blood on his fingers.

I looked at Maya. Twenty feet away, bleeding into snow. Her heartbeat a moth's wing against glass.

The bond screamed.

My shadows wrapped around Silas in restraints—wrists, ankles, throat. Black tendrils sinking into frozen earth. I threw him at the converging Sentinels. "Secure him."

I dropped to my knees in her blood.

"Maya."

Her eyes were open. Unfocused. Pupils blown wide. The venom had spread from her shoulder across her chest, shutting down organs in systematic cascade.

"Kael..." Blue lips. Distant voice. "Cold."

I pulled her into my lap. My shadows curled around her with desperate tenderness.

"Stay with me."

"It's okay." She tried to smile. Doctor voice. "Just a scratch."

"It's not a scratch."

"No." A rattling breath. "It's not."

Her heartbeat: *thump......thump..........thump*. The gaps stretching, each pause a door opening onto silence.

"I can save you. But you die first. Real death. Your heart has to stop. And there's no guarantee you'll come back."

Her hand found my wrist. Ice-cold fingers gripping.

"Do it."

"You need to understand—"

"I understand." Her eyes focused with iron clarity. "I'm dying anyway. I can feel it." Blood at the corner of her mouth. "Want to live. With you."

"It'll hurt."

"Already hurts."

"It'll be terrifying."

"Already terrified." Her grip tightened. "Choose you. Choose us."

The bond pulsed between us.

I bit my wrist open and pressed it to her lips. "Drink."

Weak, choking swallows. My blood running over her chin. She gagged and kept going.

The virus transferred through the bond—a warm pulse, a lock clicking. My blood in her veins, rewriting her biology. This would keep the venom at bay and let me drain her without being affected.

Her head fell back against my arm. I cupped her face. Freezing skin.

"I'm sorry." My voice cracked. "I love you."

Her eyes held mine.

I lowered my mouth to her throat.

I bit down.

The taste of her blood flooded my mouth—copper and warmth and home. Through the blood I tasted her fear, her determination, her love pouring through the bond in a wave that almost made me stop.

I didn't stop.

I drank.

Her heartbeat slowed. *Thump.........thump...............thump.*

She made a small, frightened sound. Her body tensed—instinct fighting decision. Her fingers dug into my arm. Holding on.

The blood flowed slower. Her skin went corpse-pale. Her breath slowed to long gaps. The venom mixed with my blood on my tongue, bitter and chemical.

Her eyes were wide. Full of terror and pain and trust. She trusted me to bring her back.

I wasn't sure I could.

Thump.

Long silence.

Thump.

Longer silence.

Her breath stopped. A final exhale. Her fingers loosened. Muscles losing signal, nerves going dark, the body shutting down system by system.

Thump.

Silence.

Nothing.

I pulled my mouth from her throat.

She stared at the sky. Brown eyes open, fixed, empty. No breath. No heartbeat through the bond—just a void where her life had been.

Her body settled with the specific, final weight of the dead. She went slack. Heavy. Gone.

My shadows wrapped around her and wouldn't let go. Raw, desperate need to keep her close, keep her mine even though mine was a corpse with my blood on her lips and her blood on my mouth.

"Come back to me. Please."

The garden was quiet. Sentinels had Silas restrained. Draven stood at the perimeter, then turned away. Walked into the stone barrier and disappeared. He couldn't watch this.

The Sentinels dragged Silas toward the treeline and he stopped mattering entirely.

Maya's face in moonlight. Still. Perfect. Dead.

Running footsteps. Heavy breathing. Human heartbeat pounding—panic.

Raj came through the gap at full speed, skidded on bloody snow, and stopped.

He stared at his sister's body in my arms. Her slack face. Her open eyes. The blood pooling beneath us.

His mouth opened. Closed. "Is she—"

He couldn't finish.

I looked up at him. Tears on my face. Hands shaking. The void in the bond where her heartbeat should have been.

"She's dead." My voice. A stranger's voice. "She has to be. It's the only way."

8
Death's Door

Kael

I shadow-traveled with a corpse in my arms.

The darkness folded around us through cold passages between points of light. Her head lolled against my shoulder. Her arm hung limp, gold bangles catching no light.

Raj's footsteps behind me. Running. Human speed. He'd arrive minutes after I did, following the address I'd thrown over my shoulder before the shadows swallowed us.

The warehouse materialized. I laid her on my bed.

Black sheets made her skin look ash-gray and waxy. I arranged her with shaking hands—smoothed her hair, straightened her blood-stiff scrubs, centered her head on the pillow.

She looked like she was sleeping.

She wasn't.

I took her hand. Her fingers were cold. Not winter-cold—the deeper, final cold that leached warmth from my own skin. The cold of a thing that used to be a person.

I'd carried this cold before, centuries ago. A charge I'd failed to protect.

Maya's hand felt the same.

My shadows wrapped around her, searching for the pulse that wasn't there. They moved in restless patterns, confused, seeking the heartbeat they'd orbited for days.

The bond was a phantom limb. Where I'd felt her hum against my soul, only dead static remained. I reached through it, pushed into the silence.

Nothing pushed back.

The warehouse door slammed open fifty minutes later.

Raj appeared, breathing hard. Snow on his boots, coat half-unzipped, face blotchy and tear-streaked.

He stared at his sister on my bed.

His jaw worked. No sound. He crossed to the other side, knelt, and pressed two fingers to Maya's throat. I watched him search for a pulse he wouldn't find. He tried again. Pressed harder. Moved to her wrist, then her chest, palm flat over her sternum.

His hand started shaking.

"There's nothing." His voice cracked. "She's—Kael, she's gone."

"She has to be. The virus only works on the dead. She'll come back."

The words hung between us—muffled, unconvincing. A prayer dressed up as certainty.

Raj sank into the corner chair and dropped his head into his hands.

Fifteen minutes. Nothing.

Her skin had cooled another two degrees. I brushed my thumb across her knuckles—back and forth, a rhythm that meant nothing, accomplished nothing, that I couldn't stop.

"How long?" Raj asked the floor between his feet.

"Forty-five minutes on the fast end. Two hours on the slow end."

"And if it's more than two hours?"

"It won't be."

I didn't say what we both knew. The answer was lying on my bed in blood-soaked scrubs.

Thirty minutes.

Raj paced—up, down, window, back. His heartbeat filled the silence, too fast, too loud, counting off the seconds his sister spent dead.

I hadn't moved. My hand around hers. My shadows around her body. My eyes on her face.

I killed her. I put my mouth to her throat and drank until she went limp. Felt the last beat of her heart and kept drinking.

And now she's dead.

And she might stay dead.

The gold bangles on her wrist caught the lamplight. I'd watched her push them up her forearm when she worked, heard them clink when she gestured.

I adjusted them, straightened them. A useless gesture when the alternative was screaming.

Forty-five minutes. The earliest conversions woke at forty-five minutes.

Maya didn't wake.

"What does it feel like?" Raj's voice scraped raw. "For her?"

"I don't know. She's dead."

"But the virus—it's doing something?"

"It should be."

"Should be." He stood, arms crossed, knuckles white. "You killed my sister on a should be?"

I looked at him. Twenty-two years old. His sister's body on a bed and all the facts in the world couldn't make this make sense.

"She chose this."

"She was dying. People say all kinds of things when they're dying."

"She chose this."

He turned away, pressed his forehead against the wall. His shoulders shook silently.

Come on. Come on, come on, come on.

At fifty-two minutes, Theron Adamas walked in without knocking.

He looked at Maya's body. At me. At the blood crusted on my hands.

He pulled a chair to the opposite side of the bed and sat. Storm-gray eyes met mine across Maya's body.

"I heard. Silas is in custody. How long?"

"Fifty-two minutes."

"Nova took ninety-three. I counted every second."

My jaw tightened. "Nova was healthy. Silas's claws had toxin. What if it damaged something the virus can't repair? What if I was too late?"

"Then you honored her choice." His eyes held mine. "Sometimes that's all you can do, and the universe doesn't care."

Not comfort—truth. The specific, terrible truth of someone who'd sat where I was sitting.

"That's not good enough."

"No. It isn't."

Three men and a corpse and the slow bleeding of minutes.

Seventy-five minutes.

Raj broke—sliding down the wall to the floor, shoulders heaving with sobs that came from somewhere deep and structural. A twenty-two-year-old kid watching his sister die twice in one night.

Theron crossed the room, lowered himself beside Raj, and put a hand on his shoulder. Just held on.

I didn't look away from Maya's face.

My shadows tightened around her, pressed against her sternum, her ribs, her still heart.

Nothing.

"Come back to me." My voice cracked. "You promised you'd haunt me. Don't break that promise. You chose this. You chose us." My thumb moved across her knuckles. "Please."

The word disappeared into cold air.

Ninety minutes. Past average. Past typical. Deep into she might not come back territory.

"Theron. You said Nova took ninety-three minutes."

"Yes."

"Three more minutes."

He held my gaze, didn't say what we both knew—that Nova's conversion meant nothing for Maya's.

But I clung to it. A number. A target.

I leaned down, pressed my forehead against hers. "Come back. Please. I can't do this without you. I won't."

Ninety-three minutes. Nothing.

Ninety-five. Nothing.

One hundred minutes. One hundred and two.

I killed her. The thought settled into my bones, becoming the foundation of every minute I'd live from this point forward.

Raj had stopped crying, sat staring at nothing. Empty.

My shadows pulled back from her body—not a decision, a surrender.

One hundred and seven minutes.

Her right index finger twitched.

My entire body locked. Everything froze on that single point of contact.

Did I imagine—

It twitched again.

"Maya?"

Behind me, Raj scrambled to his feet. Theron stood, eyes locked on the bed.

Her hand twitched—the whole hand this time, fingers curling inward.

Her eyes snapped open.

Solid black from corner to corner. No whites, no irises, no pupil. Two pools of absolute darkness staring at the ceiling without recognition.

My shadows surged toward her, and for the first time, something pushed back through the bond.

Pain.

Raw, white-hot, cellular-level pain flooding through the bond in a wave that nearly knocked me sideways. The virus, waking up. Tearing through dead tissue, ripping it apart, rebuilding it.

Maya screamed.

The sound wasn't human—too high, too sustained, rattling the windows. Raj stumbled backward, hands over his ears.

Her back arched off the bed, spine bowing, every muscle firing at once. I caught her shoulders and pinned her down. She thrashed with more-than-human strength.

"It hurts! MAKE IT STOP!"

I gathered her against my chest, held her while her body seized, pressed my mouth against her hair.

"I know, baby. I know. I've got you."

9

Transformation

DAY 1 — THE BURNING

MAYA

Fire.

Not metaphorical fire. The kind that melts steel and turns bone to ash. Every cell igniting at once, a chain reaction with no off switch.

I screamed. Or I was already screaming. Time had stopped making sense somewhere between dying and waking up.

Kael's arms around me. His mouth against my hair, words I couldn't parse through the roar of my own blood cooking in my veins.

The virus moved through me like acid, sliding through arteries, branching into capillaries, touching every organ with fingers of molten glass. Each one flaring white-hot as it began tearing me apart.

"Kill me." The words scraped out. "Please. Kael."

His arms tightened. His shadows spread across my skin—a cold compress of living darkness. It helped for half a second before the fire ate through it.

NIGHT 1 – THE BREAKING

My femur snapped.

I knew the sound—the wet-stick crack of a long bone giving way. I'd set them in the ER, told patients rate your pain on a scale of one to ten while calculating dosages.

Ten. The answer was ten multiplied by the screaming void of a body remaking its own skeleton.

The bone broke and reformed. The virus optimizing my skeleton for a predator's body without anesthesia.

My ribs went next. All of them, cracking inward and snapping back in rapid succession. I couldn't breathe. My voice was gone, screamed away. I grabbed Kael's arm and dug my fingers in, mouth stretched wide in a silent howl while my vertebrae cracked one after another down my spine.

C1 through L5. I felt every single one.

DAY 2 – THE DYING

My mother stood at the foot of the bed.

White coat. Stethoscope. Reading glasses pushed into her hair. She looked exactly like the last time I'd seen her alive.

She wasn't angry. Worse—disappointed. "Rule one, Maya. You don't get emotionally involved." Her ghostly hand gestured to Kael. "What do you call this?"

"Mom. I'm sorry."

"You were supposed to save lives, not throw your own away."

The room warped. Cemetery. Gray headstones. A fresh grave with an open casket and when I looked down—my face. My body. My mother's gold bangles on a dead woman's wrist.

Raj stood at the edge. Crying.

"Stay here." Kael's voice. Against my ear. "Stay with me. Don't leave me alone in this."

His shadows wrapped around me—anchoring. Pulling me back from the grave, from my mother's ghost.

The cemetery dissolved. Kael's face above mine—silver eyes red-rimmed, shadow tattoos writhing.

"Kael."

"I'm here."

My eyes burned. Something shifting, recalibrating. I blinked and the world turned red. Gold. Green.

"Her eyes are cycling." Theron's voice. "The virus is settling on her final form."

I pressed my face into Kael's chest and breathed in the smell of him—shadows and night air and blood. And underneath, something fading.

My own scent. Disappearing.

NIGHT 2 — THE HUNGER

Blood.

Human blood—hot and alive—somewhere above me, and my body moved before my brain engaged. Hands grabbing, mouth open, fangs bared.

Shadows caught me. Wrapped around my wrists and yanked me back. I thrashed and snarled because that heartbeat upstairs was everything.

Something pressed against my mouth. A blood bag—cold, dead, wrong.

I drained it in three swallows and screamed for more, for real blood.

"Not from them." A voice. "From me."

Skin against my lips. A wrist. Beneath it—blood. Not human. Something older and deeper, flowing with ancient power.

I bit down.

The blood hit my tongue. Iron and ozone and impossible power. I tasted his fear. His love. His three-hundred-year loneliness and the night he found me and the way his hands shook when he drained me in the snow. Guilt and devotion and the raw flavor of a man who would let me drain him dry.

The feral animal in my chest quieted, settling.

The world came back. The warehouse. The bed. A face above mine—silver eyes, blood running from the wrist I'd torn open.

"Kael?"

His face broke into relief. "I'm here. Always."

DAY 3 — THE SETTLING

The fire banked to embers. A bone-deep ache humming through every cell. But compared to the burning, the breaking, the hunger—this was manageable.

I opened my eyes.

I could see every thread in the lampshade. Every dust mote. Every crack in the ceiling. I could hear Raj's heartbeat upstairs, traffic outside, a dog barking three blocks away. Hundreds of heartbeats hammering against my new ears.

"Too much." I pressed my palms over my ears. It didn't help.

"You'll learn to filter." Kael beside me, his face in perfect clarity.

"How much longer?"

My voice came out different. Richer. Resonant.

Relief flooded his face. "Soon. You're almost there."

I reached for his hand. My arm moved too fast, fingers closing with force that made him wince.

"Sorry. Everything's calibrated wrong."

"It'll take time." He lifted my hand to his mouth, pressed his lips to my knuckles. "But you'll get there."

NIGHT 3 — THE COMPLETION

The final wave hit at midnight.

Not fire. Not breaking. Not hunger. Every system in my body locking into place, clicking home, the virus finishing its work with one last surge.

I screamed—not suffering. Completion. A single clear note ringing through the warehouse, through my bones, through the bond connecting me to Kael.

Then silence.

My body went still. The ache vanished.

I stopped breathing.

I waited for panic. It didn't come. I didn't need air. My chest lay flat and quiet, the absence of breath as natural as anything.

Darkness. Peace.

Real peace. The first I'd felt in three days. In two years. Maybe ever.

Quiet.

10
Awakening

Maya

Eyes open. Gold.

Predator gold—the color at the center of a flame right before it eats everything around it.

I could see the reflection of my irises in the lamp's glass base fourteen feet away. Count the filament coils inside the bulb—seven. Read the manufacturer's stamp on the brass fitting.

My doctor brain tried to categorize this. Enhanced visual acuity, estimated 20/5 or better.

My not-doctor brain just screamed.

I lay still. Not breathing. My chest didn't move. My lungs sat inside my ribs like deflated balloons and my body had zero complaints.

Then sound hit—a wall of noise slamming into my ears. I flinched hard enough to rattle the bed frame.

Raj's heartbeat. Upstairs. Sixty-eight beats per minute. The rhythm I'd listened to through a stethoscope when he had pneumonia at six, when he broke his collarbone at twelve, when Mom died and I needed something to count.

My mouth flooded with saliva.

I pressed my tongue against the roof of my mouth and felt fangs. Retracted but there, tucked against my gums like switchblades, pulsing in time with my brother's heart.

That's your brother. That's Raj. He is not food.

Beyond his heartbeat: traffic, car stereos, a dog barking blocks away. Heartbeats layering on heartbeats until the city became a single massive organism and I could hear all of it.

"Too much." My voice scraped out, a resonance underneath like someone had strung a cello string through my vocal cords.

"I know."

Kael. Beside the bed. I turned my head and—

Oh.

Silver irises ringed with darker gray. Three days of stubble—I could count individual hairs. Shadow tattoos coiling across his collarbones, writhing in patterns that matched his breathing.

And on his left wrist: my bite mark. Two crescents, still healing.

I remembered the taste of him.

My fangs pressed against their sheaths.

"How do you feel?"

The words were buried under the lamp's electrical hum, the whisper of fabric, a pigeon's heartbeat on the roof. "I can't—" I pressed my hands to my ears. "I can't turn it off."

Relief flooded his face—raw as a wound. He'd sat here through three days of my screaming and breaking and dying, and he hadn't left.

I needed to sit up.

My abs contracted and the world blurred and I was across the room, back against brick wall, bare feet on concrete.

"Ow."

Kael's eyebrows climbed.

"You're stronger now. You have to learn control."

"I moved twelve feet in—how long?"

"About a quarter second."

"That's not physically—" I stopped. Laughed. "Right. Vampire. Physics doesn't apply."

Blood. On the sheets. On Kael's wrist. In the scratches down his forearms.

"I need." My fangs slid free, pressing against my lower lip. "I need..."

Kael stood. Slow. Deliberate.

He held out his wrist. No hesitation. Just his arm extended, silver eyes on mine.

"From me. Only me until you learn control."

I crossed the distance. Three steps, human speed, measured. His wrist came up and I could see the veins beneath his skin, blue-purple rivers carrying blood that smelled like midnight and ozone.

My fangs sank in.

His blood hit my tongue and the world expanded.

It tasted of devotion. Of terror. Of a love so absolute it felt like its own kind of dying. Everything he couldn't say, poured directly into my veins.

I drank until the hunger banked. Until Raj's heartbeat upstairs stopped sounding like a dinner bell and went back to being my brother's pulse.

I pulled back. Licked the wound closed and wiped my mouth.

"That was...intense."

Kael's mouth twitched. "You'll get used to it."

"Not sure I want to."

The smile landed. And his shadows reached for me.

I reached back—not with my hands, but with something new. The shadows responded. Peeled away from his skin and wound around my fingers like cats.

I turned my hand. They slid between my fingers, up my wrist, cool and alive. Curious. Happy. Playful.

"I can feel them." My voice cracked. "They're part of me now."

Kael's jaw worked. His eyes bright and wet.

"They chose you before I did. That night in the ER. They reached for you and I didn't understand why."

The shadows pulsed against my wrist. Warm.

I turned away—too much, too raw—and reached for the doorknob.

Metal crunched. The knob crumpled in my grip like a beer can.

"I just—"

"You're stronger now."

"You mentioned that."

I walked to the bathroom, measuring each step. The light was off but I could see everything—white tile, chrome fixtures, the crack in the mirror.

The mirror.

I stopped.

Same bone structure. Same long black hair. Same cheekbones, nose, mouth.

Not the same eyes.

Gold. Not the warm brown I'd inherited from my mother. Gold, the color of amber, of a predator's iris catching light.

My skin had changed too. Still brown, still mine, but smooth in a way skin shouldn't be. Every scar gone—the burn on my forearm, the chicken pox mark, my appendectomy scar.

I pulled Kael's shirt aside and checked my shoulder. Where Silas's claws had torn through muscle and bone. Where I'd bled out.

Nothing. Smooth. Unmarked.

My body reset to some platonic ideal. The faint lines around my eyes—gone. I looked twenty-five. Would look twenty-five forever.

My mother's gold bangles glinted on my wrist. Still there. The one thing that survived.

"I'm...I'm beautiful."

Kael appeared in the doorway. His reflection behind mine, silver eyes finding gold in the glass.

"You always were. Now you see it."

"I'm dead." I said it flat, sitting on the bed. "I died. I felt it."

Kael sat beside me. Close but not touching.

"And you came back. You chose this. Chose me."

"I know I chose it. I'm processing."

He waited.

Dead. My heart didn't beat. My lungs didn't fill. I would never grow old. I would watch Raj get wrinkles and gray hair and eventually—

"Can I still practice medicine?"

"Yes. Night shifts. There's a whole vampire medical world. Clinics, trauma centers. They need ER doctors."

I stared at him.

"You're telling me there are vampire hospitals."

"And they need ER doctors."

The pressure behind my eyes wasn't tears.

"I can save people for centuries now. Not just years. My mom had thirty-two years of practice. I could have thirty-two hundred."

Something in my chest expanded.

I laughed. Wet and cracked and gold-eyed and happy.

A knock on the doorframe.

Raj stood there in his U of M hoodie, trying so hard to be brave it made my chest hurt.

"You look...different. Same but not."

His heartbeat climbed. He smelled like sleep and anxiety and underneath: blood.

I pressed my tongue against my fangs.

"I'm still me. Just...more."

Raj's chin trembled. I loved him so fiercely that shadows spilled from my wrist and reached for him.

They brushed his hand. He flinched—then didn't pull away.

"I'm okay." I stood slowly, measured. "I promise. I'm happy."

"That's—" He wiped his eyes. "That's the first time you've said that since Mom died."

I closed the distance. Wrapped my arms around him with the care of someone handling glass, every ounce of new strength leashed and controlled.

He hugged me back. Tight. His heartbeat hammering against my silent chest.

Over his shoulder, I caught Kael's eye. The bond flared—his relief in my chest, his pride warming my limbs.

I looked down. Shadow marks. Dark, shifting lines tattooed across my left wrist, matching the ones on Kael's right. Moving in sync.

Raj pulled back. "Your eyes are really cool, by the way."

I laughed. Richer, with that cello-string resonance, but me.

Kael taught me to drink from a bag. It tasted like gas station coffee compared to his wrist. I drank three and didn't complain.

He explained the basics—blood daily at first, then weekly. Sunlight like a migraine. Human food fading over months.

My doctor brain took notes. I was already building a treatment protocol.

"You're taking mental notes."

"Someone should write this down."

The corner of his mouth lifted. "Theron's wife said the same thing."

The rooftop air hit my skin. Forty degrees, northwest, carrying rain and exhaust and the Mississippi River three miles south.

The cold didn't bother me at all.

Minneapolis spread below. Same skyline I'd seen a thousand times.

Not the same at all.

I could see a couple arguing four blocks away. Hear a bartender pouring draft beer. Smell Thai food—each spice distinct.

And heartbeats. Thousands of them. A city full of fragile, burning-bright human life.

"It's overwhelming."

Kael stood beside me. The bond hummed between us—my awe answered by his centuries-old sorrow, his calm steadying my frantic new senses.

"You'll learn to filter. Give it time."

Time. I had centuries of it now.

I reached for his hand. Slow. Measured. My fingers closed around his with exact human pressure.

His hand tightened. The shadow marks on our wrists pulsed in unison.

"Thank you. For choosing this. For choosing me."

He turned. Silver eyes finding gold. His hand came up, tucking my hair behind my ear, fingers tracing my jaw.

"Always." His thumb brushed the corner of my mouth. "In every life, I'd choose you."

I leaned into his hand. Closed my eyes. Opened them again because I didn't want to miss a single second of seeing the world this way—sharp and bright and terrifying and beautiful, all of it at once, forever.

11

Forever Starts Now

MAYA

Six months. That's how long it takes to go from screaming on a bed while your bones rebuild themselves to holding a newly converted vampire's hand and saying, "I know. You're almost through."

The girl on the clinic bed gripped my hand with granite-crushing strength she didn't know she had yet, eyes shifting from black to amber. "It feels like dying."

"It is dying. And then it's not. The other side is worth it."

Her Shadow Twin paced outside—boots on tile, ragged breathing, weight shifting every time she made a sound. I checked her vitals. Cell regeneration: 94%. Bone density: complete. Neural pathway reconstruction: 87% and climbing.

She'd wake tomorrow and break at least two doorknobs before lunch. I had a pamphlet for that. *So You're a Vampire Now: A Practical Guide for the Recently Dead.* Raj said the title needed work. Kael said it was perfect.

Her grip loosened. Real sleep pulled her under.

Her Shadow Twin appeared in the doorway. Dark circles, wrinkled shirt, the wild look of a man who'd killed his girlfriend to save her.

"She's settling. She'll wake tomorrow confused and hungry. Be patient. Let her break things."

"Is she—"

"She'll be fine. Six months ago, that was me on that bed."

Relief crumpled his face. I left him and walked down the corridor, dropping my gloves in the biohazard bin.

My phone buzzed. *Outside.* —K

Two words. Every shift. 182 times now, and the flutter behind my ribs hadn't faded once.

The black SUV sat at the curb. Kael leaned against the passenger door, silver eyes catching the streetlight, shadow tattoos moving down his forearms.

In four hours, he'd be my husband.

"How was the shift?"

"Conversion case. She'll wake up tomorrow." I kissed him, his hand settling on my hip, shadow marks pulsing in sync. "Her Shadow Twin is a wreck."

"They all are. I was."

"You talked to me. That's different." The seat was warm—heated, the way he did every night. "I could hear you. Somewhere in the dark, something that was still me knew you were there."

His shadows stirred. Through the bond: warmth so profound it felt like sinking into a deep, calm ocean.

The warehouse smelled like home—my shampoo and his weapon oil. My running shoes beside his tactical boots. My mother's photograph beside a shadow-forged blade from Theron.

Raj sat on the couch eating cereal from a mixing bowl. "My sister's getting vampire-married today. Do I call it a bonding? A bitey commitment ceremony?"

"Bonding ceremony. And don't lead with 'bitey' in your toast."

"Theron thinks I'm funny."

Kael's mouth twitched. "You're funny."

"He's being polite."

"Also, Priya's coming. She's wearing green."

"Your girlfriend from House Sapphira is coming to our House Adamas ceremony?"

"Theron's using my charm for diplomacy. Priya is a bonus."

I threw a pillow at him. He caught it, grinning.

God, I loved him. Same kid brother who'd cried into my shoulder six months ago, now cracking jokes in a vampire warehouse at four AM. Raj made the impossible family.

❦❦❦❦❦

The blood-red dress fit perfectly. Silk. Floor-length. Low back showing the shadow marks climbing my spine. Mother's gold bangles on my left wrist.

Gold eyes. Brown skin holding light. Hair down in waves I'd never bothered with during residency.

Tonight I wasn't Dr. Reeves. I was just a woman about to marry the man she'd literally died for.

KAEL

Velvet Shadow's main hall glowed with candlelight. Stone archways. Vaulted ceilings. Draven's masterwork.

I noticed none of it. Only Maya. She walked toward me, and every Sentinel instinct went silent. Her.

My shadows reached for her before I could stop them, curling around her wrist.

"Hi."

"Hi."

"You look like the reason I survived."

"That's either the most romantic thing you've ever said or the most codependent. I'm going with romantic."

Theron stood at the front. Nova beside him. Two converted Shadow Twins.

The ceremony was old. Theron spoke words in a language older than the Houses, and shadows rose from the floor, weaving between Maya's hands and mine like dark thread.

"I choose you." Maya's voice carried clear and steady. "Every day. Forever."

The shadows flared. Gold and silver light where they intersected.

My turn. My voice cracked on the first word.

"I choose you. Every day. Forever. In every life. In every shadow. You."

The binding completed. Our shadow marks blazed. The room erupted.

I looked at Maya. My wife. My mate. My Shadow Twin.

I deserve this. Not a question. A fact, settling into the foundation of me like bedrock.

MAYA

The reception filled Velvet Shadow with sound and movement. I ran my fingers along the warm stone wall.

"This is incredible. Who built this?"

"Draven. Took him fifty years." Kael handed me blood wine. "Blood Architect's masterwork."

"Is he here?"

"Draven doesn't do crowds."

I scanned the room. Then saw him—at the far edge, half-swallowed by an alcove. Broad shoulders in dark green. Emerald eyes watching with the stillness of someone who'd spent centuries perfecting the art of being present without participating.

"Your friend looks lonely."

"He's always alone. Says he prefers it."

"No one prefers being alone. They just stop believing they'll find someone."

Through the bond: a ripple of recognition. Kael had been that man in the alcove.

Draven's head snapped toward the window. His emerald eyes flared. Then he was gone.

"His vault. Below the building. He retreats when the world gets too close."

I wondered what he'd sensed out there.

Outside Velvet Shadow, a woman raised a camera.

Click. The eastern facade. Click. The roofline. Click. The service entrance.

Professional. Methodical. She moved along the building's perimeter with the efficiency of someone who understood that architecture told you everything about its vulnerabilities.

She didn't notice the stone beneath her fingertips hum when she touched the wall.

The warehouse rooftop. Minneapolis spread below in ten thousand points of light.

Kael sat beside me on the ledge, seven stories of empty air beneath our feet.

"Regrets?"

"None. You?"

"None."

Silence. The good kind.

"She'd be proud. I'm saving people. Forever now."

"More. We could build the clinic. The conversion trauma center. And the Sentinel training program—medical modules for bonded pairs."

"And travel. You've had three centuries and barely left the Midwest."

"I was working."

"Working and brooding. For three hundred years." I leaned into him. "I want to see everything."

"Then we'll see it. All of it."

His lips found my temple. My jaw. The corner of my mouth. I turned into him and the kiss was unhurried, certain.

His shadows wrapped around us. Mine rose to meet them, weaving together above our heads, blocking the city's light, leaving nothing but stars.

"I love you."

"Forever."

Two vampires on a rooftop, wrapped in shadows and starlight. Bonded. Whole. Home.

Beneath Velvet Shadow, Draven Emeris stood among his treasures in a vault carved from bedrock. Paintings from the Renaissance. Roman coins. A medieval tapestry.

He pressed his palm against the eastern wall. The stone was warm. Residual heat—not temperature, but presence. Someone had touched the other side.

His shadows stirred. Restless. Reaching toward the warmth with a hunger he hadn't felt in a very long time.

Emerald eyes glowed in the dark.

"Someone's watching my building."

About the author

V.A. Browning writes contemporary romance that sizzles with workplace tension and authentic emotional depth. Her passion for storytelling was born from years of being a voracious reader who devoured romance novels by the stack, always searching for stories that balanced smart, capable characters with the messy, wonderful reality of falling in love. After spending over a decade in the hospitality industry, she discovered that the high-pressure, fast-paced world of hotels and restaurants provided the perfect backdrop for the kind of intense, slow-burn romance she loves to read—and write.

Her novels draw directly from her professional experience, bringing insider knowledge to stories about driven characters who find love in the most unexpected places. V .A. specializes in workplace romance featuring competent, passionate people who are masters of their professional domains but complete disasters when it comes to matters of the heart. She believes the best love stories happen when two people let their carefully constructed armor crack just enough to let someone else in, and she's particularly drawn to exploring how cultural heritage and family legacy shape the way we love.

When she's not crafting the perfect enemies-to-lovers dynamic or perfecting a hero's swoon-worthy declaration scene, V.A. can be found in her cozy home office overlooking her garden, usually with a diet coke within arm's reach and her two rescue dogs—a mischievous Whippet named Louie and a silly Boxer named Rocky—sprawled at her feet. Her ideal Sunday involves farmers market visits for fresh flowers and artisanal coffee, followed by afternoon sewing sessions where she creates quilts from vintage fabrics she's collected over the years. She's a firm believer that the best stories, like the best meals, are meant to be savored slowly.

V.A. is passionate about representing authentic cultural experiences in her work. She lives in Oklahoma with her two dogs, an ever-growing collection of fabric scraps, and enough romance novels to stock a small bookstore. She's currently working on her next novel, another workplace romance that promises to deliver the same blend of professional competence, cultural richness, and irresistible romantic tension that readers expect from her stories. When readers ask her about her writing philosophy, she always says the same thing: every reader deserves a happily-ever-after that feels both swoon-worthy and real, featuring characters who are passionate, flawed, and deeply, beautifully human.

Learn about all the books she has available at www.nickannypublishing.com/va-browning/

Shadow Bound Mates - About The Series

WELCOME TO THE SHADOW BOUND MATES SERIES

Vampires. Fated mates. A series of books where immortal grumps meet the humans who refuse to swoon on command.

In the Nyx Universe, vampires don't sparkle—they brood, kidnap, and are hilariously bad at feelings. Each has spent centuries searching for their Shadow Twin, the one person immune to their compulsion, compatible on every level, and destined to drive them absolutely insane (in the best way).

What to expect:

- Fated mates who argue their way into forever
- Banter so sharp it could draw blood
- Protective vampires with unique magical abilities
- Spicy scenes with supernatural flair ()
- Romcom tone with genuine emotional beats
- Conversion arcs (death, rebirth, and happily immortal after)

- Found family across the series
- Guaranteed HEAs for every couple

Each book is a standalone romance featuring a different vampire House and power set, but characters weave through the series, building a world where Shadow Twins find each other, build clinics, start rebellions, and occasionally save Minneapolis from vampire civil wars.

Start with any book, fall in love with them all.

Find them all at books.vabrowning.com

www.ingramcontent.com/pod-product-compliance
Lightning Source LLC
LaVergne TN
LVHW051013080826
845145LV00009B/2597

* 9 7 8 1 9 7 1 1 0 9 0 4 6 *